PILOT PUPS

By **Michelle Meadows**

Illustrated by **Dan Andreasen**

Simon & Schuster Books for Young Readers
New York London Toronto Sydney

For Gerry and Mel, my amazing parents—M.M.

For Katrina—D.A.

Michelle would like to give special thanks to Chase, Richard, and Joanna Feliz.

SIMON & SCHUSTER BOOKS FOR YOUNG READERS
An imprint of Simon & Schuster Children's Publishing Division
1230 Avenue of the Americas, New York, New York 10020
Text copyright © 2008 by Michelle Meadows
Illustrations copyright © 2008 by Dan Andreasen
All rights reserved, including the right of reproduction in whole or
in part in any form.
SIMON & SCHUSTER BOOKS FOR YOUNG READERS is a trademark of Simon & Schuster, Inc.
Book design by Einav Aviram and Karen Hudson
The text for this book is set in Minya Nouvelle.
The illustrations for this book are rendered using Winsor and Newton oil paints on cotton canvas.
Manufactured in China
10 9 8 7 6 5 4 3 2 1
CIP data for this book is available from the Library of Congress.
ISBN-13: 978-1-4169-2484-5
ISBN-10: 1-4169-2484-1
* first edition *

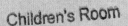

Start the engine,
buckle up.
Down the runway . . .

Pilot Pups!

Rolling faster,
lift up high.
Soaring, roaring—
to the sky.

Canines cruising,
in control.
Searching, searching—
on patrol.

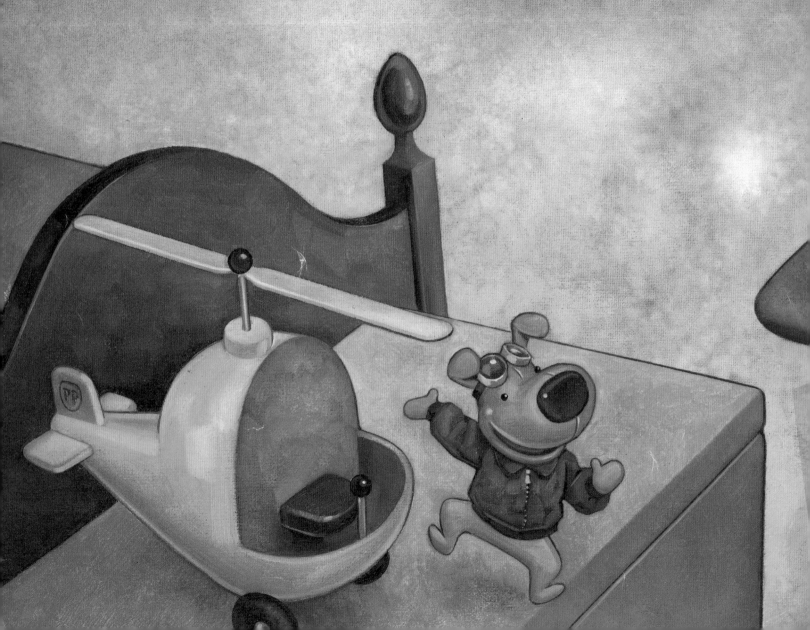

Bumpy, jumpy,
rocky ride.

Climbing higher,
start to glide.

Watch out for the
mountaintop!
Curving, swerving,
sudden drop.

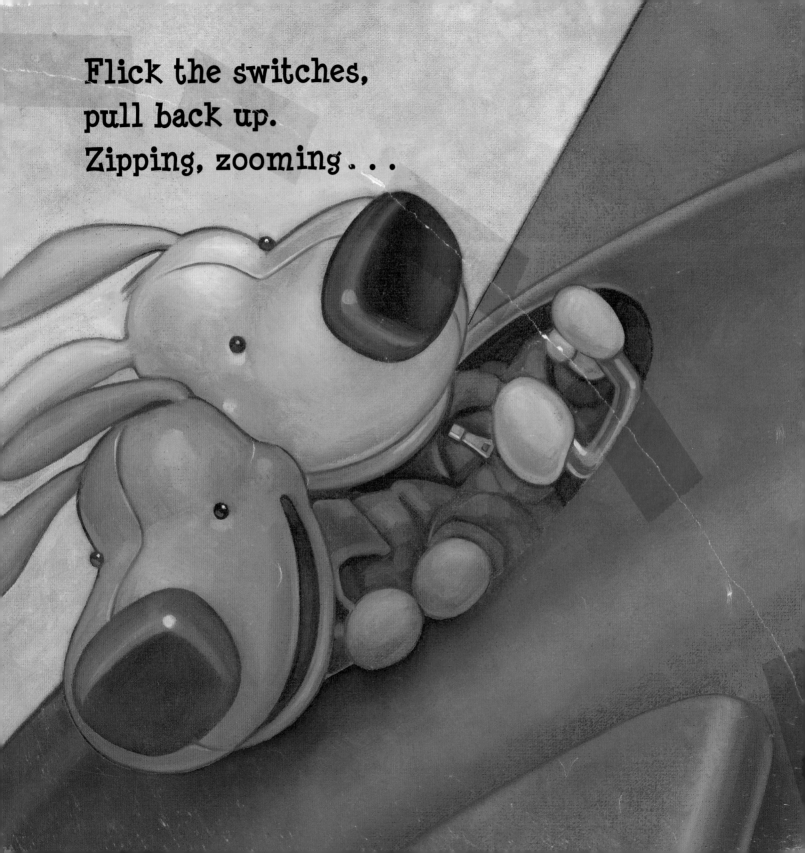

Flick the switches,
pull back up.
Zipping, zooming . . .

Up and over,
in between.
Double-check the
radar screen.

Pilots see a
patch of fog.
"Hit the lights!"
shouts Captain Dog.

Scan the valley,
cruise the creek.
Flying round
a pointy peak.

Smoky signal
rising up.
Dart in closer . . .

Pilot Pups!

Stranded buddies
in big trouble.

Call a chopper
on the double!

Whizzing, whirring,
spin and shift.
Drop the rope and . . .

lift, lift, lift.

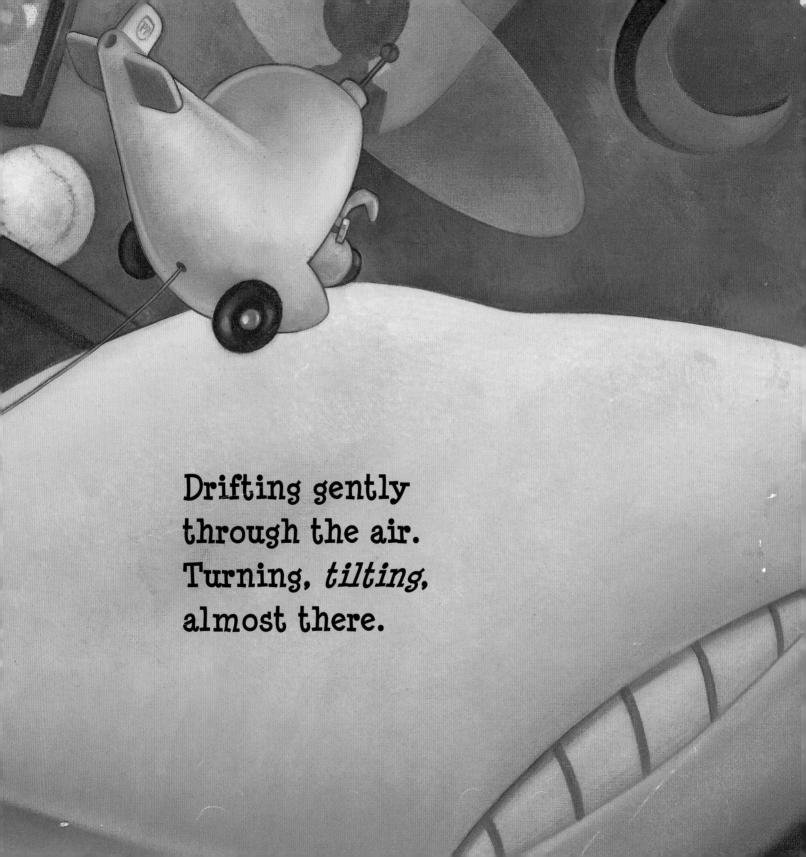

Drifting gently
through the air.
Turning, *tilting*,
almost there.

Pups glide softly
to the ground . . .

Everybody's
safe and sound.